P9-CLD-917

J.V. BROWN LIBRARY
6801 9100 116 225 3

DISCARD

Up and Down on the Merry-Go-Round

Up and Down on the Merry-Go-Round

By Bill Martin Jr.
and John Archambault

Illustrated by Ted Rand

Henry Holt and Company · New York

One for the money,
two for the show,
three to make ready
and here we go
to the merry-go-round,

Up and down,
around and around
on the merry-o-merry-o
merry-go-round.

This painted pony
is just for me,
I'm *whoooooooooopee!*
happy as can be.

A prancing pig,
a dancing bear,
an ostrich loping,
and a hopping hare,
gliding, striding,
everyone riding,
side by side,
giddy-up! giddy-up!
I'll ride the wind,
they'll never catch up.

My jumping horse
has a flying mane
and a bridle made
of purple chain.

Galloping, galloping,
wild and free,
there's my mother,
she waves at me.

Everyone riding,
everyone riding,
up and down
around and around.

30

Floating up
to my own dream land,
my heart keeps time
with the big brass band.
Oom-pah-pah,
melody surrounds me,
Oom-pah-pah,
dizzy-all-around me.
Cymbals clash!
Trumpets sing!
I'm high in the clouds,
my horse has wings.

Galloping through
the mirrored sky,
strings of stars
are whirling by.

There's my father,
Oh no! Gee whiz!
He's eating my popcorn,
he thinks it's his!

Everyone riding,
everyone riding,
up and down
around and around.

A clown comes through
the jungle thicket
with a hand outstretched
to take my ticket,
winking, blinking,
hear the bells a-tinkling.
Where, oh where,
look again! look again!
which little pocket
did I put it in?

A burst of joy
each time around,
up and down
on the merry-o—
Oh no!
it's slowing down . . .
Not now,
merry-go-round . . .
don't stop now . . .
keep going . . .
keep going around . . .
around . . .

When I grow up,
I'll be the clown
who never stops
the merry go-round . . .
the mer-ry-o
m e r r y - o
m e r r y
g   o   o   o   o   o

roooouuuund.

To Janice and Chad

Who have given me
a string of stars
for my own dream land.
J.A.

Published by Henry Holt and Company, Inc.,
115 West 18th Street, New York, New York 10011.
Published in Canada by Fitzhenry & Whiteside Limited,
195 Allstate Parkway, Markham, Ontario L3R 4T8.

Library of Congress Cataloging in Publication Data
Martin, Bill.
Up and down on the merry-go-round /
by Bill Martin Jr. and John Archambault ;
illustrated by Ted Rand.
Summary: In this rhyming story, children describe
the sights and sounds of riding on the merry-go-round.
[1. Merry-go-round—Fiction. 2. Stories in rhyme.
I. Archambault, John. II. Rand, Ted, ill. III. Title.
PZ8.3.M4113Up 1988
[E]—dc19 87-28836

ISBN 0-8050-0681-8 (hardcover)
10 9 8 7 6 5 4 3
ISBN 0-8050-1638-4 (paperback)
10 9 8 7 6 5 4 3

Henry Holt books are available at special discounts
for bulk purchases for sales promotions, premiums,
fund-raising, or educational use. Special editions
or book excerpts can also be created to specification.

First published in hardcover in 1985 by
Henry Holt and Company, Inc.
First Owlet paperback edition, 1991

Designed by Marc Cheshire
Printed in Mexico